Disney's CHRISTMAS MAGIC

Written by Elizabeth Spurr

Illustrated by Disney Storybook Artists

Disney PRESS

NEW YORK

First Edition
1 3 5 7 9 10 8 6 4 2
ISBN 0-7868-5383-2
For more Disney Press fun, visit www.disneybooks.com

TABLE OF CONTENTS

ANDY'S CHRISTMAS PUPPY

On Christmas morning, the toys waited anxiously for the Green Army Men's report. The men had been sent on a recon mission to find out (1) what Andy had got for Christmas and (2) if he had received any toy that he would love more than them.

The army men had no sooner set up their operation

than they heard the sound of barking. "Wow!" cried Andy. "A puppy!"

"We're dead!" said cowboy Woody to his friends. "Do you all know about puppies?"

Buzz Lightyear, the space ranger, looked blank. "Never heard of them."

"Puppies are some super-toy that's almost human,"

said Woody. "I mean, they wiggle and run and bark, and they don't need batteries. Kids are crazy about them."

"Whoa!" said Buzz.

"Not only that, they eat," said Woody. "I mean eat and swallow. But worse that that, they chew."

"Like Sid's dog?" asked Rex. The timid dinosaur trembled.

Cruel Sid, who used to live next door to Andy before they moved, often let his dog chew toys.

"Now, fellas," said Bo Peep. "You know Andy wouldn't let anything hurt you. He takes good care of his toys."

The group stood in shocked silence.

Just then Andy burst into the bedroom, carrying the

dreaded puppy in his arms. He set the puppy on his bed, but it immediately bounded off, making the rounds of the room, sniffing at each toy and knocking over the Green Army Men. They were helpless to defend themselves.

Andy's mother came in, carrying a wicker dog bed and two bowls that said DOGGY.

"I'm not sure this is the best idea," she said, "having

Buster sleep with you."

"He'll be good, I promise," said Andy.

"Any problems with him and he goes back to the laundry porch."

Andy put the dog in the basket and said, "Stay!" But the minute he left the room, the puppy raced after him.

"The puppy's going to ruin Andy's room!" said Woody. "And who knows what he'll do to us! This calls for drastic action."

"All we have to do is teach the little fella some

manners before he has a chance to rip us to pieces," said Buzz. "Or I can just fire my laser at him."

"That's it, Buzz!" said Woody. "The part about teaching the puppy some manners. We can help Buster find his way to obedience school."

They gathered in a circle to plan their strategy. "We need to figure out the bad things a puppy would do," said Woody. "Then we'll help him do them."

"How about spilling his food and water?" said RC Car. "I can do that in one run."

"I can dent the furniture," said Buzz. "Make it look like the puppy chewed it."

"We all can help mess up the room," said Bo Peep.

They quickly set about putting the room in complete disarray.

They no sooner got

themselves strewn across the floor than the puppy came

bounding in. *Whap! Zip! Zap!* Sure enough, he took each

toy into his mouth, shook it violently, and tossed it. The

air rained soldiers, dolls, and stuffed animals. The toys

got the puppy into such a frenzy that he skidded about

the room, chewing

everything in

sight.

Whiz! RC Car

headed for the

food and water

bowls. Buzz flew at the puppy, who had Rex in his mouth.

Andy's mother heard a crash and came into the room. "Oh, dear!" she said. "I knew it."

Andy spent Christmas night mopping up the mess and placing each toy on its proper shelf. At bedtime he pleaded with his mother, "What fun is a puppy if you can't sleep with it?"

"You have Woody and Buzz," she said.

"They aren't soft and warm," said Andy. He stayed awake listening to his puppy's cries. When he finally drifted off to sleep, a single tear slid down his cheek.

The toys spent a miserable night. Between Andy's being upset and the puppy's whines from the laundry porch, they got no rest. Woody, who loved Andy dearly, could not bear to think he had made

the boy so unhappy.

The next morning, Woody gathered the toys for a meeting. "Hey, guys. Maybe we  were a little hasty. I, for one, don't want Andy to be unhappy. After all, our whole reason for being is to make Andy smile."

"But what if the puppy chews us?" said Rex.

"If you all stay on the shelf where you belong," said Woody, "the puppy can't reach you. Only Buzz and I, here on the bed, are in danger."

The toys behaved themselves and stayed on their shelves. When Andy forgot to put one away, somehow it managed to get back to its safe place.

Andy's mother remarked how neatly he was keeping his room and how well Buster was behaving.

"Maybe then," said Andy, "you'll give Buster and me another chance."

And she did.

Each night, snuggled next to the puppy, Woody wondered if his days were numbered, if  one morning at sunrise, he and the dog would have a showdown. He liked to think he'd be brave. He would give his all for Andy's happiness.

But that day never came. The first time the puppy nosed Woody, Andy rapped the dog gently across the muzzle. "No, Buster!"

Before long, the toys befriended the dog, who was not vicious, and they realized he was just young and in need of training. That was soon taken over by RC Car, Buzz, and the Green Army Men.

But no one felt as close to Buster as cowboy Woody.

DISNEY'S TARZAN®

CHRISTMAS IN THE JUNGLE

Jane looked around the tree house with a melancholy face.

"Do you feel all right?" asked Tarzan. "You don't seem your usual cheerful self."

Jane forced a smile. She was fine. Why shouldn't she be? She, Tarzan, and her father, Professor Porter, loved their life in the jungle, surrounded by their ape family and the other animals.

They had added rooms to the tree house until it was now almost like a mansion. And Tarzan was the bravest, strongest, kindest man a woman could ever ask for. Then why did she feel so blue?

She glanced at the calendar. December 23. "No wonder!" she said. "Without the change of seasons, I completely forgot. It's almost Christmas."

"So it is," chuckled Porter, who had been napping in his rocker.

"I'm going to miss it," sighed Jane.

"Christmas?" said Tarzan. "If you need a Christmas, I'll be glad to get you one." He would go to the ends of the earth to make Jane happy.

"Let me explain, Tarzan," said Jane. "Back home in England, where Daddy and I come from, Christmas is a holiday."

"A holiday," repeated Tarzan with a puzzled look on his face.

"Yes," continued Jane. "It's a day of celebration, the most beautiful day of the year."

She went on to describe snowfall and sleigh bells, pine trees and packages, tinsel and tender roast goose.

"I don't think I could bring you a snowfall," said Tarzan.

Jane brightened. "But maybe we can do the rest. Well, sort of, anyway."

"I don't see why not," said Porter. "Christmas is more than snow and sleigh bells. It's a time to share with friends. And we have plenty of them." He looked out toward the jungle.

The sun was setting beyond a glassy pond where

elephants were bathing. Among the trees that lined the shore they could see the dark shapes of their ape family.

As evening shadows began to lengthen, the darkness was filled with the sounds of jungle creatures: chirps, screeches, growls, and roars. Jane smiled and turned to Tarzan.

"As Father said," she explained, "Christmas is a time of

sharing. Our friends
need a Christmas, too!"
She told him her plan.

The next day, assisted
by their ape family, Jane
and Tarzan went through
the jungle, picking
fruits and nuts. Tarzan
found a small tree in the

forest, which, with Jane's help, he shaped into a Christmas tree. They decorated the tree with garlands of bright berries. When all was finished, Tarzan set a paper star on the top.

"There is still something missing," said Jane. "Our tree doesn't have any lights."

"There are a few candles left," said Porter.

"That's a wonderful idea, Daddy," said Jane. "And I have another idea."

On Christmas Eve she and Tarzan captured hundreds of fireflies in small jars, leaving holes in the jar lids for the insects to breathe. They hung a jar on each tree limb. The tree sparkled with light.

From the tree house they looked down on their outdoor tree, where the animals were gathered, gazing in wonder. There were turtles and crocodiles; birds, elephants, and hippos; rhinos and zebras. There were graceful antelopes and awkward wildebeests; and, of course, the families of apes and baboons.

Into their midst strode the mighty cats—the lions, the leopards, the cheetahs. A hush fell over the jungle as the animals moved back to allow the fierce, powerful beasts to approach the tree.

"Look!" cried Jane. "They're all together around the tree, like . . ."

"It can't be!" said Tarzan.

". . . like one big happy

family," said Jane.

The lions, leopards, and cheetahs sat on their haunches, staring at the tree, then curled up like pussycats beneath its branches.

At that moment, a solitary bright star appeared in the sky, shining directly above the paper star of the decorated jungle tree.

"I do like Christmas," said Tarzan. "It's . . . it's like magic."

Porter looked down at the peaceful animals in amazement. He lit his pipe and shook his head. "Why can't Christmas last all year round?"

Walt Disney's Bambi

THE WONDERFUL WINTER TREE

Bambi awoke one morning to find a fluffy white blanket covering the whole world.

"This is snow," said his mother. "It means winter is upon us."

"Snow?" said Bambi. He walked in a circle and felt the cold snow crunch under his hooves as he made tracks round and round. "I like snow."

"Snow is pretty to look at, but winter can be hard," said his mother. "Especially when we animals can't find food."

Just then Thumper called to Bambi from a frozen pond. "Hiya, Bambi! Why dontcha come sliding?

Look, the water's stiff!" Bambi nuzzled his mother

good-bye and pranced off to join his friend.

Flower came over to see what was going on. "You wanna come skating?" Bambi asked. "The water's stiff."

"No, thanks," said the skunk. "I'm ready to settle down for a long winter nap."

He called to the squirrel, who stood in the hollow of his oak tree. "The pond is stiff. Come sliding."

"Thanks, but I'm storing nuts for the long winter."

The chipmunk was in his nest, and the bear was asleep in his cave. Bambi went to the pond alone, where he found Thumper whooping it up with his rabbit friends.

For Bambi, the skating was not as much fun nor as easy as it looked. After dozens of flops on the ice, he was both bruised and hungry. So, Bambi set off to find his mother.

"Mother, I'm hungry," he said.

He looked for a patch of
grass, but all was covered over.

"Today we'll have to search
for our dinner," she said.

Following his mother,
Bambi poked through the snow
until he thought his nose would
freeze. They finally uncovered a mound of greens.
Bambi's mother watched over him as he ate.

Then they curled up in the thicket for a long nap,
their bodies huddled against the chilly air. Before

falling asleep, Bambi turned to his mother. "Winter sure

is long, isn't it?"

Day after day the animals spent most of their time in

search of food. Bambi and his mother, often followed

by Thumper, scoured the forest, sometimes with little

luck. "Mother," asked Bambi, "is this why the birds fly south, and why our other friends sleep through the winter?"

His mother nodded yes, and gently nuzzled him.

The sun had set. It was almost time for sleep, but Bambi had found little to eat except some bitter bark. Then, at the edge of the valley he and his mother came upon a wondrous sight—a tall, snow-covered pine tree, draped top to bottom with strings of berries and

popcorn. From each branch hung a ripe green apple.

"Mother!" cried Bambi. "Look!"

Slowly, cautiously,

his mother drew closer.

"It seems too good to be

true," she whispered.

"What is it, Mother?"

asked Bambi.

"The most beautiful

tree I've ever seen," she

said. "He must have known that this was your first Christmas, Bambi."

"Who, Mother? Who?" Bambi was so hungry, he could almost taste those juicy apples.

"Santa Claus," explained Thumper.

"Santa Claus?" said Bambi. "Who's that? And what's a Christmas?"

Thumper and Bambi's mother explained that Santa was a jolly, magical elf who visited just around the time of the first snowfall each year. They told Bambi all about how he delivered presents and holiday cheer, and about his reindeer and sleigh.

"It was Santa who hung those berries and apples," said Thumper. "And put that star on the top."

After calling the good news to other animals, Bambi and his mother, along with Thumper, gathered to share the feast.

As they ate, they noticed a bright star in the heavens, a star like the one atop the pine tree. And as it shone, a hush settled over the valley,

the sound of silence, of peace on earth.

When he gazed at the star, Bambi felt warm inside, and his heart swelled with the hope that spring would soon arrive.